If you're happy

Published in the United States of America by Star Bright Books, Inc., New York.
Published simultaneously in the United Kingdom by Oxford University Press.
The name Star Bright Books and the logo are trademarks of Star Bright Books, Inc.
Star Bright Books may be contacted at www.starbrightbooks.com.
9 8 7 6 5 4 3

Hardback   ISBN 1-932065-07-5   LCCN: 2002013692

Library of Congress Cataloging-in-Publication Data

Ormerod, Jan.
If you're happy and you know it! / Jan Ormerod & Lindsey Gardiner.
p. cm.
Summary: A little girl and various animals sing their own versions of this popular rhyme.
ISBN 1-932065-07-5
[1. Animals--Fiction. 2. Happiness--Fiction. 3. Stories in rhyme.]   I.
Gardiner, Lindsey. II. Title.
PZ8.3.O718 If 2003
[E]--dc21

Printed and bound in China by Imago

2002013692

and you know it!

Jan Ormerod   Lindsey Gardiner

Star Bright Books

New York

One day a little girl felt

"If you're happy and you know it, clap your hands.

If you're happy and you know it, clap your hands –

If you're happy and you know it, clap your hands.

clap, clap!

happy. So she sang,

If you're happy and you know it,

and you really want to show it..."

"No, no, no," said the small brown dog.

"If you're happy and you know it, wave your tail – swirl, twirl!

If you're happy and you know it,
whisk your tail around to show it.

If you're happy and you know it,
wag your tail!"

"My tail is rather insignificant,"
said the elephant. "So I sing,

If you're happy and you know it,
flap your ears.
If you're happy and you know it,
flap your ears –

flip,   flap!

If you're happy and you know it,

flop your ears around to show it!"

"Ridiculous!"
cried the crocodile,
whose ears were very
small indeed.

"If you're happy and you
know it, snap your teeth.

If you're happy and you know it, snap

your teeth - snip, clip!

If you're happy and you know it, flash those big white teeth to show it!"

"Or clack your beak?"
called the toucan.

*"If you're happy
and you know it,
clack your beak —*

click,

clack!

If you're happy and you know it,

snip
and snap
your beak
to show it!"

"Pathetic,"
said the gorilla.

"If you're happy and you know it,
beat your chest.

If you're happy
and you know it,
pound your chest –
boom, boom!
If you're happy
and you know it,

thump your
hairy chest
to show it!"

"Hip, hop," said the kangaroo.

"If you're happy and you know it, jump and bump.

If you're happy and you know it, jump and bump –

ping, pong!

If you're happy and you know it,

boing boing along
to show it!"

"If you're happy and you know it, shouted the parrot.

"If you're happy and you know it, you should

ya

you should **screech!**"

scream –

hoo!

If you're happy
and you know it,

shriek
and shrill,

scream
and yell.

If you're happy
and you know it,
you should screech."

The hyena giggled.

"If you're happy and you know it, have a laugh.

If you're happy and you know it, say tee-hee, ha-ha, ho-ho!

If you're tickled and you know it,
chortle, cackle, chuckle, titter.
If you're happy and you know it,
have a tee hee hee."

"So when I'm happy," laughed the little girl, "I can do my own thing!"

"That's right," they all cried.

When you're happy and
When you're happy and
Beat your chest,
clack your beak,
giggle screech,
Do your
YA

you know it, do your thing.
you know it, smile and grin.
flap your ears,
snap your teeth,
boom boing.
thing
HOO!

For Lynda, Jen, and Chrissa, BE HAPPY! – L.G.